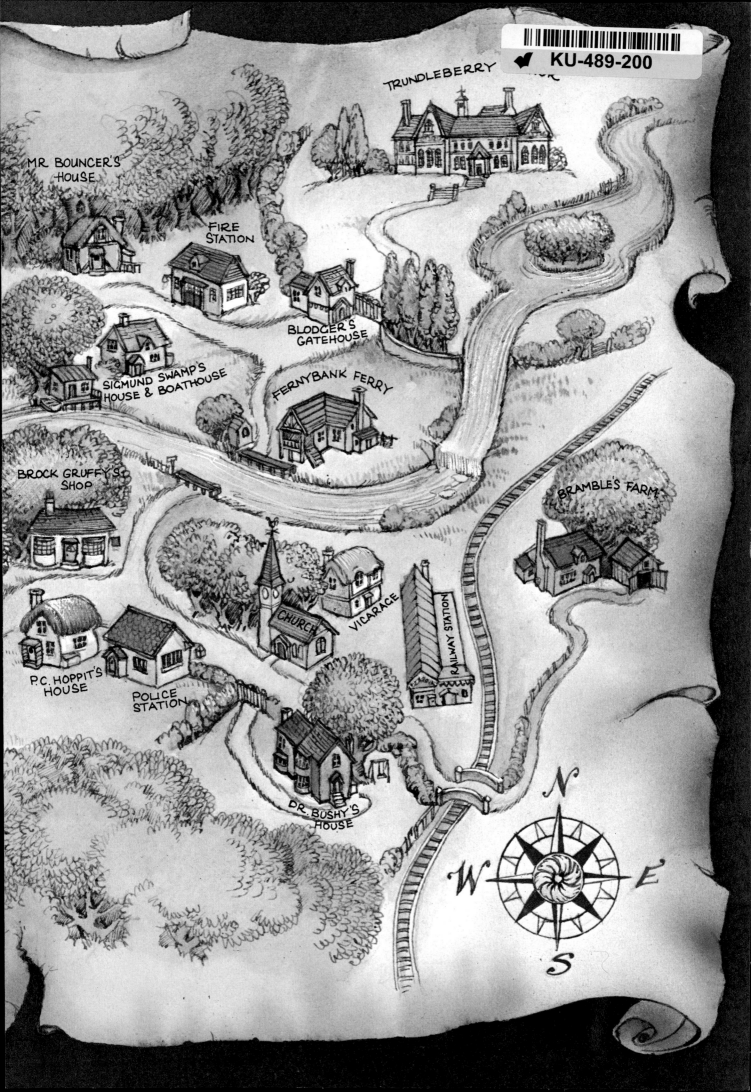

This book belongs to:

....

Sigmund's Birthday Surprise

Written & Illustrated by
John Patience

THIS EDITION PUBLISHED 1991 BY COLOUR LIBRARY BOOKS LIMITED,
GODALMING BUSINESS CENTRE, GODALMING,
SURREY GU7 1XW (0483) 426266
© PETER HADDOCK LIMITED.
PINFOLD LANE, BRIDLINGTON, U.K.
PRINTED IN ITALY
ISBN 0 86283 862 2

The birds were singing and the early morning sunshine was glinting through the trees, as Mr Periwinkle the Postman came driving along the lane in his post van. Normally Mr Periwinkle did his rounds on his bicycle, but this morning he had an especially large birthday present to deliver to Sigmund Swamp. It was a long wooden crate, and rather strange snorting noises were coming out of it! The crate was very heavy and Sigmund had to help Mr Periwinkle to carry it into the house. "It says, 'From Uncle Oscar to Sigmund on his birthday' ", said Sigmund, reading the label. "I wonder what it can be."

Carefully, Sigmund began to prise the lid off the crate.
As he did this the snorting noises from inside grew louder
and louder, until at last the lid popped open and out
crawled an enormous crocodile! In the twinkling of an
eye, Mr Periwinkle rushed out to his van and drove
away, and Sigmund scrambled up on top of a cupboard.
Meanwhile, the crocodile began to gobble up the poor
toad's breakfast. He was very hungry. In fact, he hadn't
had a bite to eat since he left the Amazon jungle, where
Uncle Oscar had caught him!

8

Having polished off Sigmund's breakfast, the crocodile still felt hungry and went off looking for more. He made his way through the garden and slid into the river Ferny. As he swam past the school, the children were playing football. Spike Willowbank gave the ball an extra hard kick which sent it flying over the playground wall. It would have landed in the river, but the crocodile caught it in his mouth and made a nice little snack of it.

11

When the crocodile reached the dam at Mr Croaker's watermill, he climbed out of the river and wandered around until he came upon Mrs Prickles, who was hanging out her washing.

"Good gracious," cried Mrs Prickles, almost jumping out of her shoes. "It's a crocodile!" And she scurried into her house and bolted the door behind her. As for the crocodile, he took a fancy to the washing and ate the lot, sheets, pillowcases and all.

13

Mrs Prickles's washing had been very tasty, but now the crocodile sniffed the air and caught a scent that was absolutely delicious. It was coming from the bakery where Mr Acorn had just finished baking a batch of cream buns and jam tarts. What a feast they made! The crocodile ate every last one of them, smacked his lips, and then devoured a shelf of crusty loaves.

"Go away at once," shouted Mr Acorn, waving his rolling pin angrily. But the greedy animal didn't leave until he had eaten everything in sight.

By this time, Sigmund had informed P C Hoppit about the escaped crocodile, and together they set out to track him down. They hadn't been searching long when Sigmund heard an odd little sound coming from behind a tree.

"Boo-hoo. Boo-hoo-oo."

It was the crocodile and he was crying.

"Dear me," whispered P C Hoppit. "What can be the matter with him?"

"I expect he's feeling lonely," replied Sigmund. "After all, he is the only crocodile in Fern Hollow."

"Yes," agreed P C Hoppit. "I think I'd better telephone Poppletown Zoo to come and take him away. There are bound to be other crocodiles at the zoo to keep him company."

Before long, a Zookeeper arrived in a large van with a
cage on the back. On the Zookeeper's instructions the
cage was baited with a tray of hot swiss rolls, supplied by
Mr Acorn. Then everyone hid themselves and waited.
The crocodile was still crying behind his tree, but when he

caught the delicious smell of the swiss rolls he quickly
perked up and crawled out to investigate. The moment he
was in the cage the Zookeeper leapt out from his hiding
place and locked the door.

"Hooray!" cried everyone.

"Mmmm," said the crocodile, munching the swiss rolls.

It turned out that Sigmund's Uncle Oscar had intended to send the crocodile to the zoo in any case, instead of which he had sent them a crate of Amazon honey, which was really Sigmund's birthday present. He had simply mixed up the labels. The crocodile settled in nicely at the zoo, where Sigmund visited him from time to time and fed him a few of Mr Acorn's cream buns!

Fern Hollow

MR CHIPS'S HOUSE

MR WILLOWBANK'S
COBBLER'S SHOP

MR CROAKER'S WATERMILL

STRIPEY'S HOUSE

SCHOOL

THE JOLLY VOLE
HOTEL

RIVER FERNY

MR ACORN'S
BAKERY

MR RUSTY'S HOUSE

MR PRICKLES'S HOUSE

POST OFFICE

BORIS BLINKS'S
BOOKSHOP

MR TUTTLEEBEE'S
SHOP

MR THIMBLE'S
TAILOR'S SHOP

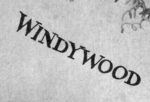
MR TWINKLE'S
HOUSE

WINDYWOOD